S0-DVF-075

This book belongs to:

Copyright 2019 by Beatriz Rare

Cover and illustrations by Beatriz Rare

April 2019, Irvine, CA

Seymour the Lemur

Deals with anger

Book 1

Ever since Seymour was a little baby, he ate bugs and leaves like other lemurs. But his favorite food has always been fruit.

Seymour likes bananas and pineapples, but there is one fruit he loves the most.

He goes crazy for oranges!

One time, a lemur named Dennis did something that made Seymour very angry.

He took Seymour's precious orange

and put it in his mouth!

Seymour became so angry that something happened. An anger monster appeared on his shoulder. The monster told Seymour to scream and shout mean things at Dennis. Seymour knew he should not listen but...

Seymour shouted and screamed mean things anyway.

RAHHHHHHH!

All the lemurs ran away.

His anger monster told him to stomp through the jungle and unleash his anger.

Seymour screamed at every animal he saw.

He shouted at the hippos, "You are too BIG!"

The hippos felt sad.

After that, Seymour passed a group of toucans.

He screamed at them, "Your beaks are too LONG!"

The toucans felt bad.

Soon a little sloth got in the way of Seymour.

Seymour yelled at him, "You are too SLOW!"

The sloth was afraid.

After a while, Seymour was sad because he realized how badly he had behaved. He should have never listened to his anger monster. He knew what he had to do now. He needed to apologize.

The anger monster didn't want Seymour to apologize, so Seymour had to fight his way over to the sloth.

"I'm sorry I called you slow. There's nothing wrong with that."

The sloth happily forgave him.

Seymour went back to the toucans.

"I'm sorry I said your beaks were too long.

There's nothing wrong with them."

Most of the toucans appreciated the apology.

Seymour returned to the hippos.

"I'm sorry I said you were big. There's nothing wrong with that."

They accepted his apology and forgave him.

Finally Seymour went back to the other lemurs, and he apologized.

poof

That last apology made the monster disappear!

Dennis decided to apologize as well for taking Seymour's favorite food.

He handed Seymour back the orange, but it had a bite missing!

Seymour started to feel angry again, but this time he controlled himself.

But Dennis was only joking! He had a new orange ready for Seymour.

They both laughed together.

Seymour joined Dennis and the others, and all the

lemurs were happy.

They ate fruit together as they watched

a big, ORANGE sunset.

Other books by the author:

Diaries of a Dragon
Beatriz Rare

Clark is scared of the dark
Beatriz Rare

THE ENDLESS FART
Beatriz Rare

32562703R00022

Made in the USA
San Bernardino, CA
15 April 2019